The Little Green Notebook

Notes About Love & Other Things

Dalton Hessel

Printed in the United States of America

First Printing: November 2017

Dalton Hessel

P.O. Box 1264

Hayward, WI 54843

Facebook: Dalton Hessel's Writings

Instagram: @hessel_themanintheballcap

#thelittlegreennotebook

Back cover photo : Copyright © 2017 Tim Young

For my future wife.

CONTENTS

ACKNOWLEDGMENTS

Thank you to my sister, Alli. You encouraged me to write and modeled it like no other when we were growing up. Thank you to my mom and step mother for reading books constantly. It has rubbed off on me over the years. Thank you Natalie for editing this book. I definitely owe you a ton of cookies from Sweet Martha's at some point. Thank you to my teachers and professors who have guided me along this journey. A special shout out to Professor Hollars and Dr. Berchini at the University of Wisconsin-Eau Claire for encouraging me to continue writing and helping me hone my craft. I still have a long ways to go, but your help is something that I can't thank you enough for. Thank you to the friends and family that have reached out to me over social media about how my writings have helped you. Your support doesn't go unnoticed. Thank you Backroads Coffee of Hayward for not kicking me out for spending what must have seemed like hours in your coffee shop while writing this book. Finally, thank you to the women I have loved and to the women I have lost.

Author's Statement

Human connection. We long for it through relationships with friends, family, significant others, and sometimes even strangers in passing. The reason why I write is to try to build that instant connection with someone. Even if I may never meet you before, I want you to know the kind of person I am through my writing. Most days, I'm a hopeful romantic, but other days I am an adventurer, a traveler, a brother, a son, a teammate, and an old man inside of a twenty two year old's body. We often don't speak out loud what we are feeling internally because we are afraid our vulnerability will make us seem weak or not level headed. Through the act of writing my thoughts and ideas down about friendships, love, sadness, anger and other things, it has allowed me to be much more of an open person. I don't know what everyone is going through. Nobody does. That is why I hunger for that human connection through my writings because it gives voice to the things we are afraid to say, but deep down we feel.

1 LIFE & OTHER THINGS

Canoe Therapy

He hadn't been in the water all summer. Other things
seemed to have occupied his time: work, sports on
television, traveling to familiar and unfamiliar places,
nights spent thinking about her. He brought the
canoe down to the dock and looked out at the water.
No other boats occupied the lake and wind did not
ruffle his shorts. Clouds filled the sky and covered the
sun periodically like a father covering his face while
playing peek-a-boo. He lowered himself into the
canoe. The water shattered like glass and echoing
ripples dispersed. He dipped his fingers in to check
the temperature. He twiddled them around and added
a little chaos to the calmness. He paddled out as far as
his arms could take him and peeled off his ball cap.
He covered his face with it and nodded off for a little
bit. Silence for a few seconds felt like hours. A loon
called next to him and brought him back to reality.

Miles and Miles

I'm driving down this road of life. It's a long journey that has many stops along the way to take photos and make memories. Sometimes I don't know whether to stop or if I should continue on my journey. Some people are worth braking for and others make me wish I pressed down a little harder on the gas. Many miles stretch down this road that I'm on and there's no clear destination in sight. I just drive. I beat my hand on the steering wheel from time to time and wonder if I am the true navigator or if He is. Maybe I will stop here or there, but it all seems incidental. There are no passengers in my vehicle...not yet. But I do not hesitate to pick up a few hitch hikers along the way.

My TV Show

Everybody I know seems to be growing older. The gray haired men at church seem to be getting up and down more slowly. Young boys that I used to help teach and coach are now taking girls on dates and driving fast cars. My friends are finding jobs, packing up cardboard boxes, and their tires are leaving their final tracks in the driveway. Rings are getting put on fingers and vows are being exchanged. Letterman jackets that were once worn throughout the hallways are getting hung up in closets and are eager to be worn again at the next class reunion. First kisses are being shared in the front seats of cars and last kisses are being made by hospital beds. I'm not bitter towards time or friends moving in opposite directions in life, but sometimes I wish they wouldn't recast characters in my life before I am ready.

In Good Time

You're not alone in your struggle. There are other people out there who may be feeling the similar pain that you are. Maybe it's not pain, maybe it is a sense of being lost or confused. Don't worry, you're not the only one sitting at that table. The questions float around, "So what are your plans? Where are you planning on living? How come you aren't in a relationship?" Nobody has it all figured out. Everybody feels that doubt. We ask ourselves, "Am I where I should be?" It's okay to have these feelings and questions arise. Pray about it. Ask God how you want Him to use you. The answer may not be immediate, but be sure to listen when that comes, however you find it. You are not alone. It's going to be okay. You're going to find your way.

Thoughts At A Car Show

They say time travel is impossible, but I think otherwise. Every time I see an old truck it brings me back to simpler times. I think back to the young boy slipping on a pair on new blue jeans and a collared shirt to go pick her up for their first date. She's up in her room getting ready for the evening while he is downstairs meeting her father. After a short, but stern talk, her father tells them to have fun, but not too much fun. He opens the door and helps her up into his truck and they enjoy a night on the town. I think back to a father and a son escaping the city with fishing poles and tackle boxes resting in the truck bed. I think back to nights spent with blankets laid down at a drive in theater. Talk to any older person and they'll tell you that they don't make things like they used to. Vehicles, homes, products and relationships were built to last. If something was broken, you'd fix it. Time travel isn't as ludicrous as one might think. One must be willing to turn back the dial.

VHS Dream

Why do we still watch Disney movies as adults? For me, watching one brings me back to simpler times. A time in which the family was all together and nothing else was important in that moment besides making sure that everyone had a spot on the couch and whether the popcorn got burnt or not. Together we found our anthems that we would sing in the yard, in the kitchen, and along with the movie as we watched it for what must have seemed like the 1000th time to our parents. The movies now serve as an escape. An escape from a society that tells us to not dream and to not long for adventure. "It's better to play it safe," they say. "Don't move to a different city. Don't take that new job. Don't date that person." Whatever the case may be. I'm not saying you have to find a magic carpet, have magical powers or something like that to make your dreams come true. What the movies taught me was that no matter what, if you believed hard enough, if you took a chance on yourself, that your tale could come true. Maybe I'm wrong, but I'd like to think the cabinets filled will old VHS tapes say otherwise.

Late Night Thoughts

I wish there was a way to gather my favorite musicians for a meal just to tell them how much they've helped me when nobody else was there.

Tourists Vs. Locals

Some people in your life are just going to be passing through. They'll stop, take a look around for a bit and then they'll be on their way. We call these people the "tourists of life". They aren't here to stay long term by any means, but they left an impact on you whether they knew it or not. Don't waste your time thinking about the tourists of life that often. They never intended to stay. They were here to take a few photos, have a good time, and then leave. No, the people you pay attention to are the "locals of life". The people that have been by your side since day one and will be there for you. These people know your value and know your worth. They see your potential and do not take you for granted. Stop trying to always please the tourists when the locals are knocking on your front door and have an apple pie in their hands.

Mini Celebrations

Enjoy the little victories of the day. The days when you're driving and you don't hit a red light. The times when someone holds the door open for you when your hands are full. The times when you let someone into traffic when they would've been stuck for a while. The texts you get in the middle of the day from friends you haven't heard from in a while. The bedtimes stories you tell your children as they seem to be captivated and lost in a world of imagination. The leftovers that are still in the fridge when you don't feel like cooking. The nights when you can relax after a shower and watch your favorite show or movie. Enjoy the little victories as you're working your way towards the big ones. They make the minor loses a little easier to swallow.

Lunch Pail

Fill my thermos full of coffee. May it wake me up on this early morning. Full my lunch pail full of ham and cheese sandwiches. May they fight the rumble inside of my stomach. Cake my hands with dirt and calluses so I know that I put in a good day's work. Fill my truck tank full of gas to get me from here to there. Fill my bank account with money to help pay off the house and to put food on the table, but don't give me anything I didn't earn. Fill my house full of good conversations with friends and family that I don't see as much as I should. Let my body ache in the evening from all that I got accomplished. Let my work ethic resound to those around me whether I know it or not. Fill me up to be poured out for I am a working man, and my work is never done.

Running To Your Arms

Near the edge of the road there sits a shoe. A small blob of gum stuck to the bottom of the sole. The gum was enough to get his shoe stuck from time to time. Laces masked with dirt and still tied. They say he ran out of them last night. They say he couldn't handle it anymore. He had to get away. The toxic friendships he had were destroying him. He no longer felt happiness anymore when he was around them. He no longer felt appreciated. The stories began to get old. Less and less real conversations happened when they were together. They were not headed down the same path anymore, so he began to run in the other direction. They don't know if his shoes came off in a fit of joy or because he was running so fast.

Stay Hungry

A mattress on the floor keeps him humble. An almost empty fridge keeps him hungry. A jar full on coins on top of the table keeps him hopeful for the future. Money may not be in his pocket, but a strong work ethic and love is in his heart. He enjoys nights with the windows open and the rain falling outside. He finds joy in striking up conversations with strangers. He takes pride in his gritty hands after a day of work. He knows that in time the house will come, the woman he prays for he will find, and that happiness is not far away. For now, he puts his trust in Lord and does not waver when the wolf growls at the door.

The Advice We All Ignore

Love your friends just a little bit harder. Stay out on
the porch just a little but later than you're used to.
Swap stories and even if you've heard a story 1000
times, listen to it like it's the first time. Hug people
just a little bit tighter. Turn up your music just a little
bit louder. Dance like no one is watching more often.
Buy a bigger ice cream cone than you normally do.
Put away your phone more often when you're with
friends and family. Take the long way home so you
have more time together to talk about life, work,
relationships, or whatever the case may be. These may
be little things that you do, the reward for living just a
little bit harder is greater than you could ever
imagine.

Longing For Home

Home. It's not always where you grew up. Home is
the place where you find your peace. You find your
happiness. You kick your feet up and your mind is at
ease. You share good conversations whether they are
exchanged like currency in the kitchen or on the
couch. It's welcoming. People come in as guests and
leave knowing that at any moment you'll be there for
them. May the dining room table be long and may the
people sitting in the chairs be many. With every pair
of shoes that are wiped off and put to rest by the
door, may a friendship be formed. May stories and
wisdom be passed on like a hot dish. Seasons change
and decorations get put up and torn down, but the
love in the home remains constant. Even though the
winter wind may frost the windows and cause the
house to creak, the door is always open.

Keep Pouring

Fill my mailbox full of letters. Fill my heart full of hope. Fill my answering machine with messages from loved ones for me to listen to when I feel sad or alone. Fill my house with good friends and laughter. Fill my belly with cheap beer and food eaten on paper plates. Fill my mornings with sunshine and my nights with a sky full of stars. Fill my photo albums with smiles, mistimed pictures and goofiness with old and new friends. Oh, just fill me up. Fill me up with love and joy.

Storms

Somebody smiled today when they thought of you. Somebody remembered a road trip because of a song they heard on the radio and it reminded them of you. Somebody used a gift you bought them today. Somebody cooked a meal today that you taught them or introduced them to. Somebody watched a movie today because you recommended it to them one time during a conversation. Don't think for one second that you don't matter. Your thoughts, your ideas, your goals, your laugh, your style, your sense of humor, the way you eat PB&J's, the way you write your name, all of these matters and more. You are loved by many. People that are close to you and people that love you from a distance, they all have one thing in common: they care about you. Storms in your life are going to come along and they will pass. Sometimes you will face them alone and sometimes somebody will come to your rescue with an umbrella. They will make you stronger through the lighting, thunder and the rain. Sunshine is on its way.

Only Human

I wish I wasn't human sometimes. I wish I didn't
constantly worry about things in my life that are out
of my control. I wish I didn't worry about the material
goods that I have (shoes, clothes, car, DVD's, etc.). I
spend money on things I don't need and then worry
about being broke. I wish that I could love without
fear or doubt. I lie awake at night and wonder if I will
end up alone. I wish that I didn't judge people by
their appearance before I get to know them. That
when I looked at a woman, the first thing to come to
my mind wouldn't be her outer appearance. There's a
lot of things that I wish I could change, but that's the
beauty of going through life as a human.

No Hands

"Look Mom, no hands!" It means to let go. To trust. To believe that you will not fall and even if you do, you'll get back on the bike again. Try letting go of the handle bars a little more often. Take a chance on a new job, buy that plane ticket, take that road trip, or talk to that one girl or guy. Along the ride there will be scrapes, cuts and bruises. You may hate your job. You don't go to work happy and each day is a struggle. People are going to fall in and out of your life and it's going to burn like peroxide cleaning out your cut. The scar will form, but you will heal in good time. Don't forget that along the ride there will be many happy moments as well. Hold onto these moments. Appreciate the sunshine and don't be afraid to let go every once in a while.

The Getaway

The camp fire was now his companion. A cool breeze ruffled and playfully shook his tent. The moon was now up in the sky and cast just enough light so he could cook the fish he caught from today. His clothes were still drying on the line after an unexpected fall into the river. He tried jumping from rock to rock like a little kid and slipped right into the rolling river. He was lucky to have caught a large rock and was able to hoist himself up. As he stoked the campfire, his mind wandered back to camping trips with his old man. Summer days spent out in the wilderness with a sun faded ball cap on and a fly fishing rod in his hands. The embers were disappearing into the starry night. This was his home away from home. No stoplights, no deadlines, no sirens, and no bills. Just a campfire and a week off of work. He was wild again.

An Evening On The Water

A man and his grandson were out fishing one afternoon. They weren't having much luck catching fish and the grandson's line got snagged on a log. He fought and tugged with all of his might until the line finally snapped on him. He threw his pole down in the boat and let a few swear words fly. His granddad picked up his pole and looked down at it. The sun was starting to go down on the lake, but there was still a little time for a couple more casts. "Let me tell you the difference between a boy and a man," the grandpa muttered. "A man respects the hand that he is dealt, but if it isn't what he likes, he busts his back to better his odds. A boy whines and complains. A boy expects things to fix themselves. A man doesn't run in the face of danger. He greets it with a smile and a clenched fist. A boy runs from anything uncomfortable and is afraid of taking chances. A man is someone who doesn't like to fight, but isn't afraid to back up his buddy outside of a bar. A boy goes around grabbing other guy's girls and picking fights with guys twice his size. A man respects his mother. A man knows how to treat a lady. A boy leaves her up at night crying wondering what she did wrong. And finally, a man fixes his own fishing pole." The grandpa handed his grandson the mangled pole and the two carried on with their evening out in the boat.

A Night Drive To The Other House That Built Me

The only thing that is the same now is the fire number. The trees that grandpa had planted have been chopped down to make room for a garage. Quite a bit has changed. I hope that the house still rings with laughter and good conversation. That the fire pit ignites on summer nights and brings families closer together with each ember that fades into the night sky. That each snow fall brings with it the crunch of fresh footprints being forged by family members old and new as they come over to open presents. That many meals are shared together and warm fresh cookies are consumed at the kitchen counter. That cartoons are watched on the living room floor with a bowl of cereal or ice cream. I wish that games are played in the front yard with greasy pizza boxes as bases for kickball. Above all, I wish that along with the many changes that come to the place that I've called "grandma and grandpas" for many years, the one thing that may never change is the community that it created. That although we may only drive past to see what it looks like every couple of years, that the memories made there with family and friends stick with us forever like a dirty joke told by grandpa.

What Society Isn't Telling You

Your beauty is so much more than what the mirror says. It's all the little things that it doesn't say. Like your ability to laugh when laughing seems impossible at the time. The way you write your name on a piece of paper. The kind of music you listen to. Your voice and how it carries throughout the house whenever you talk. You have goals and aspirations. Your perspective on the world is unlike anyone else's and it's refreshing. Don't ever settle for someone who thinks they deserve you. The best people in your life are going to be the ones that wonder how in the heck they got so lucky to ever cross paths with you. You are special. You are important. You are beautiful. Don't anyone ever tell you otherwise.

Porch

The front porch is the most essential part to any house. That's where the real conversations happen. Where philosophies are swapped and stories, both true and total B.S., are shared. Overtime, the butts sitting in the chairs may change, the grill that's provided many delicious meals (and a few burnt ones) will be replaced, and that wood is going to need to be re-stained, but the memories will never leave that porch. You carry them with you where ever you go. You share them with other people. The stories have life after death. So, when you say, "Want to go out on the porch for a while?" you are really saying, "Let me tell you a story." And whether you're hearing it for the 1,000th time or for the first time, your ears should be perked up and willing to soak it all in.

Bottle It Up

What is considered beautiful to you? To me, beauty is seeing a radiant smile across someone's face. Seeing someone wearing their favorite outfit and seeing them glow while wearing it. It's giggles and laughter on a sunny day with an ice cream cone melting in your hand as the two of you walk side by side. It's a push on the swing and running under while trying to duck under the person's feet. It's seeing someone else singing in their car and not having a care in the world. It's a pat on the back after a rough game. It's a conversation with an old friend with a beer around a campfire. There are things in this life that are so beautiful to me and I wish I could bottle them up and save them for a day when I can't seem to find it.

Listen

Listen. That's the best advice I can give you. Listen to the people in your life. Give them your full attention. So often we try to multitask or come up with a reply before the person is even done speaking. Listen to what people are telling you and then respond. Listen to your parents. They know a lot more than you give them credit for. Listen to the old men down at the VFW. They'll tell you stories about the times they were at their most vulnerable, but were able to overcome adversity in their finest hour. Listen to the married couples. The newly weds and the ones who have been with each other for what seems like forever. Each one will bring different insights for you to learn from. Listen to the people with failed relationships. They, too, will share with you a great deal of vital information. Listen to the young people around you. Their imagination runs wild and when all seems hopeless, they will still believe in you. Listen to the birds in the morning. Listen to your favorite music. Listen to the river and find peace in it. Listen to the train rumbling down the tracks. You'll never know how much you can learn from just pausing for a moment and listening to what the world has to offer.

Rain Dancing

Sad songs are for rainy days, right? Most of the time. But, what if we viewed them as days to be happy? We should take them as days to rejoice in things being washed away. Take them as days to recognize that the water is making things anew. Yes, enjoy your rainy days filled with sleeping in and watching your TV shows, but don't be afraid to run outside and dance a little bit either.

A Gift?

I'm always somewhere else other than the present. If I could be in the present, I would, but it's not that easy for me. I'm either wandering back to the past like a traveler without a compass or longing for the future like a sixteen-year-old that can't wait to be twenty-one. There gets to be a point where you start to realize if you're not in the present, you'll never truly enjoy those moments. I've missed birthdays, but I had a slice of cake. I've missed weddings, but I was at the ceremony. I've missed games, but my butt was in the bleachers. I've missed movies, but my hands were buttery from the popcorn. I've missed funerals, but I watched them lower the casket. If the present is truly a present, why do I treat it like I just got a pair of socks for Christmas?

Dalton Hessel

2 THE HEARTBREAK

Bad Habits

Maybe I'll get drunk again. Maybe I'll call you up and tell you how I feel while my conscience is intoxicated. The alcohol giving me a free ticket that I shouldn't accept, but rather tear up and throw in the trash. Maybe I'll say all of the things that I can't say when I'm sober because my heart says it's too much of a risk. A smile graces my face like the sunshine kissing the sidewalk in the morning, intimidating the cold shadows when I see you and causing the darkness to flee. Although I may not have told the joke, when you smile, your dimples emerge in the corners of your mouth like eager friends at a surprise party. I wish it didn't take alcohol for me to build up the courage that I need. You haven't misled me at all, but you feed the stray dog inside me every time I see you. I should stop accepting the food, but the taste still lingers on my tongue. I'm grieving over a love that never existed. You'll never understand the way I need you.

I Am Empty

I catch myself thinking about you with somebody else. I stick my fingers down my throat and try to throw up, but nothing comes out. I am empty. I am the empty box of chocolates left on the counter that I was planning on giving you for Valentine's Day, but I ate them all by myself. I am the unoccupied spot on the couch where you used to sit and watch movies with me. I am the box filled with your stuff in the closet, but am too lazy to throw out. I am the passenger seat now occupied by CDs to help put me in a better mood. I am empty for now, but I will be filled again.

Strangers

Strangers. Sometimes they are not people you've never met before. They are sometimes the people that used to talk to you like there was no one else around. Strangers are sometimes the people that know some of your secrets. They are the people that got to know you and your family. The people that you traveled to concerts with and made memories with. They are the people who have aged since the last photograph that you have together. Their hair may be different, they may have lost or gained some weight, they may have a new significant other, etc. The "let's hang out" texts stop. The phone calls stop. The late nights stop and they soon become strangers. "Don't talk to strangers," is what you were told when you were little, but what happens when you're older and that's all you want to do?

Weight Of The World

Sometimes the hardest thing and the right thing are the same. It's those decisions that sit in your gut and keep you up at night. The ones that have you looking up at the sky and searching for answers. The words you're afraid to let out. The message you're afraid to send. It begins to eat you up and consume your life like a hungry wolf stumbling upon a young deer. You've got to get right with your heart. Find that inner peace that you're looking so hard to find. Only then, after the words have been spoken and you feel as though you've said everything you need to say, will the weight begin to lift off of your shoulders. Stay strong and lead with your heart.

Age Of Destruction

You destroy a good woman when you think you have all of the time in the world to make up for your mistakes. The pile of dirty dishes resting in the sink leads to arguments about you not being home enough. You destroy a good woman when you keep her up at night with tears in her eyes. You destroy a good woman when you ignore her hand as it tries to connect with yours. You destroy a good woman when you mistake her kindness for weakness. You destroy a good woman when you don't value her love. You destroy a good woman when you stop chasing her. You don't put in the effort anymore like you used to when you were dating. You destroy a good woman when you no longer value the time you spend together. You are distant and you ignore the subtle things. You ignore that she hasn't touched the pasta on her plate. You ignore the fact that she hasn't smiled at you lately. You ignore the Nike duffle bag packed by the door. She becomes numb to love. She will rebuild walls around her heart that she tore down for you. Yes, for YOU. This time she will build them higher and thicker. She must protect herself now because she can't love as whole heartedly as she used to without getting hurt.

Tin Man

I'm just a man. A tin man at times without a heart. I have these thoughts of wealth and fame, but often fail to realize that I will not find the key to happiness in a pile of money. I have these thoughts of beautiful women in my bed, but know that I will not find love if I do not commit myself to one woman and give her my heart. I have these fears that I will be here and gone without making any sort of impact on the world. I struggle to find my purpose in this life. What am I put on this earth to do? I have this pain in my heart knowing that I've wronged people in my life and I may not get a chance to make it right again. I have this hope that I will be a better man of faith. I'm just a man with an alarm clock that reads that it is getting late and thoughts that keep him up at night.

Cherry Red Goodbyes

The cherry red lipstick he used to love finding on the side of his cheek or on the outside of a wine glass now coats the bathroom mirror. "Goodbye." These feelings won't walk away. They keep him up at night. They keep him from dancing with other women at the bar. She is at the forefront of his mind like a fever that keeps him in bed all day. Bed ridden and longing for her soul medicine. These feelings have him wishing he knew the right words to say either over the phone, in person or through a letter. He types out everything he wants to send to her in text, but then deletes it. He knows he has to let these feelings subside and melt away like snow erasing itself from sidewalks in the spring. Cardboard boxes graced with her name written in Sharpie are filled with old gifts, photos and t-shirts that still smell like her. His friends tell him to burn her stuff or donate it, but how can he start another fire when one is still burning inside of him?

The Replacement

Sometimes you're going to want to call them up in the middle of the night just to check on them and see how they are doing. You tap their number into your phone while you lie way awake in bed, only to quickly delete it. You'll drive by their house just to see if their car is in the drive way. Rust still accumulating on the bottom and the seat covers starting to fade a little from the sun. You know you can't go in the house like you did before, with a smile on your face, dressed up for an evening on the town, and ready to pick them up. That screen door no longer opens for you and neither does the thick white door behind it. You're not that person for them anymore. You're not the one who they call when they're having a rough week. You're not the one they think about before they make their plans for the weekend. You're not the one telling them jokes and listening to their laugh. You're not the who they are telling their friends about. (Maybe she still does, but it's usually not in a good way, now.) Your days of being that person are over. You made the decision that you longer wanted to be with that person. Yet, there's something about going from talking to that person everyday, to absolute silence that eats you up inside. You'll go out to the bars at night hoping to not run into them and their friends, but you almost wish you do at the same time. Are they happy? Is that smile still there? Did they change their hair? Maybe you're giving yourself a little too much credit by thinking that they wouldn't do all of these things whether or not they ever met you. Either way you look at it, you want to see them happier.

No Reply

Was it something I said? Was it something I did?
How come you won't talk to me anymore? You won't
text me anymore, let alone look my way when I wave
at you frantically from a distance. Steal my bike. Slash
my car tires. Leave a flaming pile of dog shit outside
of my front porch. Anything! Just do something!
Your silence seems to do more damage to me than
any of these malicious acts would.

Hey

Hey

Hey...

Sleeplessness

If you could give me back my sleep, that'd be great. I already gave you back your CDs and records. I donated the t-shirts you got me to the Salvation Army. I threw out the calendar that was etched with date nights, birthdays, and anniversaries. I took a flame to the pictures of us that were supposed to find frames. Everything of you is gone, yet you still haunt my dreams. My eyes are red as I look into the mirror and pour myself a glass of water wishing it were whiskey. I crawl back into bed and try closing my eyes one more time. I notice the closet door is open ajar…where your stuff still finds a home in a cardboard box.

Open and Close

Our doors used to open for each other, but now we are lucky to even have one another knock. I used to look forward to turning the doorknob for you. My heart was always eager to twist the knob, push it open, and see your face. A smile would be the first thing to appear on your face, usually followed by a couple of words that would get me to laugh. You spent a lot of time knocking the snow off of your boots that winter on my back porch. I spent a lot of time looking for a spot on your hooks to hang up my coat. The snow no longer lines the streets and heated blankets are no longer borrowed from a cute girl. They are only left on back porches with a note in front of a door that will no longer open.

Your Casper

I am afraid of becoming a ghost. It worries me that I will drift away and not be present anymore. No, not one of those ghosts they go hunting for on TV or one that haunts you, but one that is invisible. A ghost that wishes to be seen, but gets overlooked by life. A ghost that no longer gets the joys of human touch. I could haunt you, but it wouldn't do me any good. You'd be no more scared of me than you'd be of trick or treaters on Halloween.

Their Future

In my dreams I am beginning to see her happy. I no longer picture her crying or being mad at me. Maybe she still is, but I'm not going to entertain those thoughts. I picture her crushing hard on a man who is bright and caring. A man who has his heart in the right place and has her best interest in mind. A man who will not hide his face amidst adversity and will communicate his feelings. Let his thoughts and words not be muted in his chest. Let him fend off the river of tears from finding her eyes. Give him strength and wisdom. Help him say the right words when she is feeling sad or insecure. Let her feel like loving again and trusting someone with her heart. God knows I was a wolf in sheep's clothing, but let her find a man who isn't into wearing costumes or masks.

Nothing Has Changed

You're the tangler of headphones. You're the thief of one sock out of the dryer. You're the one to finish off the gallon of milk and not tell anybody. You're the driver that cut me off in traffic. You're the snow piled high on the top of my car when I'm in a hurry. As much as I want to, I can't hate you. Every time that I try to, only good thoughts come to my mind and I hate that. I hate that every time I look up at the stars and moon, I think about sitting on my front porch steps. I hate that every time I drive past that spot you said was your favorite that I still look at it just the same. I hate that I have to stop and think twice every time. Every time. That I pass by your house. As much as I hate these things, they're still in my head for a reason. A reason I haven't quite figured out yet.

Yet The World Carries On

My mind is somewhere else as I sit on the park bench. Crumbs from my sandwich fall onto my jeans and I am quick to brush them off. No music is coming through my headphones. Maybe it is, but I can no longer hear it. A young couple may have been pushing their baby in a stroller, but I can't tell. Everything else seems a blur. I narrow in on the text once again, "We need to talk." The text message is enough to make my hands tremble and shake. Anybody who is anybody knows that, "we need to talk," is a relationship killer. It's armed with a chainsaw and hunting for scared teenagers. The newspaper resting next to me is tossed back and forth in the wind. It flies up and I'm able to snatch it as it tries to escape the bench to wander the city streets. "No, you're staying with me," I say to it as if trying to convince it to stay and be my only friend. I spike my phone to the ground and toss the remains of it into the trash and tuck the newspaper under my arm. Everything has changed yet the world still carries on and Jack Johnson is still singing about effing surfing through my headphones.

3 THE LOVING

When I write about love and relationships, I tend to write about the thought of a perfect couple, but that's not what I expect in my own life. We all have our imperfections and that's okay. We are human. Being human isn't always easy. We are all secretly out of control in one way or another. So, when I write about relationships and love, I don't expect my relationships or all relationships to be the same way. Every love story is unique in its own way and it wouldn't be fair to expect perfection from my future wife. What I am trying to do with my stories is to have people believe in love again. Believe that it's out there. Believe that it's real.

The Student

Love. You are the best teacher I've ever had. I am a perennial student. It costs me nothing to attend class. I never stop learning when I'm in your presence. You're everywhere. You're in the grocery store, walking down the street, in the restaurant, in the church pews, at the concerts, at the stadiums, in the hospitals, and at the cemeteries. Sometimes you are a silent teacher and sometimes you're vocal. I can't escape you and I don't think I want to. All I want to do is grab a pencil and take notes.

Window Shoppers

I love window-shopping with you. The things we may
or may not buy someday keep me hopeful. Your face
glows by the light of the shop windows with your
energy electric like the neon signs. You point to the
clothes and imagine yourself in them. I imagine you in
them as well. You do an imaginary fashion show
along the sidewalk, but you carefully maneuver
around the cracks like you're a pro on the runway. We
get a few weird looks from the "cake eaters" walking
into the shops and you end collapsing into my arms,
practically dying from your own laughter. I kind of
like the fact that we don't have pockets full of cash. It
allows us to use our imaginations more and while
money would be nice to have, I would much rather
count pennies with you. Nights of emptying change
jars just to grab a slice of pizza and strut the streets
while dancing with no music don't need to stop
anytime soon.

When the Leaves Change

You asked me what my favorite season was and I will give you my honest answer. I'm happiest when the leaves are drained of their green and turn into shades of red, yellow, and orange. I smile a little wider when I'm able to pull a flannel over my shoulders and open the front door to go outside and take a walk. The air is a little crisp like when you bite into one of those caramel apples you are so fond of. I chuckle when my voice is a little hoarse after yelling in the stands at a Friday night football game. I enjoy days spent getting lost in corn mazes and tossing husks at each other. I take the best mental photos and put them on the fridge of my mind when you pick out the pumpkin. You hold it high like a trophy and you're the Queen of the Pumpkin Patch. I wish you could see the way you practically strut to the register. Your energy for life keeps me warm like the hot cider we sip on as we watch pumpkins sail into a field by a cannon. You make me fall.

She

She's the sunrise that sneaks through the blinds and warms my face in the morning. She's the crackle of the fire on a summer night as my feet slip out of my shoes and onto the dirt and grass. She's the finger of frosting that she mischievously takes off of my slice of cake. She's the pictures drawn on my back with her finger tips as we sit on the couch and watch TV at night. She's the blanket in the back seat of my car that keeps us warm as we look up at a starry night sky. And I love her. She's the pile of leaves raked up and waiting for somebody to jump into them. She's the ice cream stain, ketchup stain, BBQ stain, and any other stain that has found my clothes when we've eaten together. She's the balloon that I hold onto by the string, but give her enough slack to dance in the wind. And I love her.

Lover's Eyes

She's the frozen slushy that goes straight to my head. Or is she more like whiskey? I haven't quite figured out which one she is yet, but she hits me hard. She makes me long for the Ferris Wheel to get stuck at the top. I pray that she can't open lids on jars so I can give her a hand. She'll tell me that she loosened it up for me. My friends say I've got this "lover's eyes" look about me. What that consists of is beyond me, but I won't deny it. Mornings when she's singing Kelly Clarkson in the shower and I burst through the door to sing back up, but also to low-key brush my teeth, are the best. Random days when we hit up the thrift store and buy gifts for each other with a $5 budget is just one of the reasons why I smile when I have food stuck in my teeth. She's not my religion, but rather she has cast a spell over me. Honestly, I'm kind of surprised a letter from Hogwarts hasn't snuck in with the stack of bills. If these lover's eyes are real, never give me a reason to wear sunglasses.

The Low-key Superhero

She was able to scare away the dark. The monsters were evicted of their residency in his life. They scattered and crawled out from underneath the bed and no longer rattled the closet door. She was the warm cup of coffee for his soul. The rush to his system like a little kid already working on his second ice cream cone of the day. He was fumbling around on the floor searching for the flashlight when she approached him with her candle to light the way. He wasn't helpless without her, but she would turn his walk into a run. As she brought piles of clothes, scrapbooks, jewelry and shoes, she was also sneaking in a sense of adventure, intelligence, confidence, honesty, uncontrollable laughter and a smile. She carried with her a smile that had the ability to twist his arm and get him to do whatever she wanted. She was a borderline superhero and she knew this, but she used her powers for good...most of the time. He calls it the "blueberry waffles" smile. More often than not, he would get the smile early in the mornings as the sunshine would begin to creep through the blinds. He didn't mind the blueberry waffles smile. It was a good trade off. Simple and sweet and sometimes had the ability to set off the smoke detector in the house.

No Algorithm

Maybe we are moving together or maybe we are moving in opposite directions. It's hard to tell anymore. One day it is all smiles and laughter and the next it is short replies and messages hours later. Maybe I read this whole thing wrong like reading a map upside down. I wish the answers would come more simply like looking in the back of the book. Looking at the two of us, it doesn't make sense. It shouldn't make sense, but for some strange reason, I want it to. We are taught to protect our hearts and to protect the hearts of others. We are afraid of the uncertainty. That's the crazy thing about love: you can't calculate it out. There are too many variables in place. Who is to say who belongs with another? If love were easy, there would be no such thing as a broken heart and Ben and Jerry's would be out of business.

She Lit A Fire

Her flame is eternal. Many try to put her out with buckets of water, but she remains to burn bright. Many have tried to contain her and harness her energy, but she cannot be bottled up. Her flame may be intimidating, but she is full of warmth and love. She's comforting like a blanket under a starry night and shines even in the darkest of hours. She is not to be played with though. She can warm you, but also burn and destroy if one is not careful with her. She may spread and destroy many things in her path before settling back down. Don't worry, you'll be able to sit around her and converse again, but she will not let you get as close this time. She is a gift and one may not always be able to find the fire that she has.

We Alright

My pockets may not be deep and filled with dollar bills, but the thing inside my chest beats for you. My car brakes may squeak and squeal when we stop, but the miles we travel together are precious to me. My style may be often created out of a thrift store, but you see past the wrinkles in my shirt and fading of my flannels. Don't get me started on your style. You're going to think I'm cheesier than our fancy mac n cheese dinners, but you look good in anything. (Although half of your clothes may be my old shirts and hoodies.) Money is going to come and money is going to go. Let us not be defined by our bank account, but by the way we hold each other accountable. Let us be defined by how we treat those around us and how full our dinner table is on any given night. While I may wear a watch on my wrist, I don't keep track of time when we are together. I don't look forward to leaving you like work on a Friday. You're my favorite "hello," and my hardest "goodbye." My pockets may not be deep. My automobile may be a piece of crap. My fashion sense may be a little whack and by now you've figured out I am a fan of Weezer. My love for you is something I don't want to compare to anyone else's. I don't want to compare it to anyone in Hollywood or even the neighbors down the street.

The Seeker

Seek the woman. Seek her personality. When everything around her is telling her she's not pretty enough, let her know she is beautiful. Help her not compare herself to other women. Help her see the beauty that she possesses within her. Seek her smile and laughter when she's in a bad mood. Seek her joy and fulfillment. You should want to see her thrive. Her body may be elegant and beautiful, but one must understand that she's so much more than just a pretty face. Seek her comfort and understanding. Seek mornings eating breakfast across from each other at the kitchen table, the two of you discussing your plans for the day. Seek long walks when you come across some wildlife and the two of you enjoy nature and it's magnificence. Seek the Lord together and grow with each day. May your heart be full and may your smiles be many.

Words Are Hard

Speechless is what you leave me on most days. I wish I could tell you the things that you don't know that you do. The list I would come up with would be like one of those ancient scrolls that they used to roll out in kingdoms. The right words may not always escape my mouth and forgive me when the wrong ones do. My stupid mouth gets me into trouble sometimes, but you knew that already. When it comes to describing you to my friends and family, too many thoughts and emotions come to mind. I tell them that you're indescribable, but they tell me that's only an easy out. I give them all of the clichés about love and how you are like Christmas morning and they are satisfied with that, but there's more to you than that. While I may not say everything that you do to me, I hope they see the passion in me when I speak of you and when I am around you. I hope you see that in me as well. When words fall short, let the passion and my body language speak instead.

Endless Summer

Every kid's nightmare is having summer end. They want the days spent on the lake and the nights under the starry skies to never end. With you, my summer never ends. Yes, the season does literally end, but the feeling of young love lingers on long after the boats have been stored away and the tourists have locked the doors to their cabins. Even though the seasons may change, your warmth doesn't waver. During the fall, we tuck ourselves under blankets and spend afternoons searching for the perfect pumpkin to carve, your comfort is still present. When the bite of the winter winds keeps us indoors and we spend the day making Christmas cookies and watching "Elf"; your comfort is still present. Rain covers the windshield and I am white knuckle driving it back to our apartment; your comfort is present. The sun never seems to set on us. Your smile is what I look to and it brings me back to racing down winding backroads with our bicycles while we scream Queen songs at the top of our lungs. (I'm not going to lie, it was a little awkward when that old man saw us when he was getting his mail). When I am with you and when I am away from you, I never have to worry about summer coming to an end.

Traveling Without A Passport

You always talk about wanting to travel more. While
we may not always have money to afford trips to far
away places, let me be your escape. I'll be your escape
on autumn days with a caramel apple and a hayride.
I'll be your escape on a chilly winter afternoon with a
bowl of soup after cutting down our Christmas tree
and throwing in into the back of the pickup. I'll be
your escape when the news headlines seem too
demented to be real. I'll be your escape with a
nighttime drive to grab a Blizzard with you and walk
down Main Street. I'll be your escape with a bottle of
wine and a dinner made when you come home from
work. I'll be your escape with a drive up to Bayfield
with a mix CD I put together with our favorite songs.
Not everyday is going to be as adventurous as the last,
but I promise you that you'll want to capture these
moments.

The Waiting Game

"Just wait," they keep telling me. "Just wait and she'll come along." The hard part about waiting is the unknown and uncertainty. Did I already meet her or do I still have many years, months, weeks, days, hours, minutes, or seconds to go? I don't know why I am so eager to find her and when I do, how will I know? I imagine it coming down to things like falling in love with her laugh and smile, but there's so much more to a soul's connection than just a smile or a laugh. To me, conversation is everything. Can we talk for hours about a hypothetical movie starring us? Conversation is what I think will draw me to her. Not only her beauty, but her sarcasm, humor, intelligence and kindness. The thing is that I cannot worry about the logistics of it all. All I can do is pray for her and God's timing. Chase God first and everything will fall into place. "Just wait." It's easier said than done.

Arguing With Myself

Tell me. I want you to tell me how I got so lost in
you. Tell me why I lose sleep at night. Tell me why
my heart races and my mind relaxes whenever I see a
picture of you. Tell me why I scroll through your
social media. Tell me why I go on dates with others,
but I try to make it not work out because in the back
of my mind, I still think I have some sort of shot with
you. Please find someone else, so that I can get you
out of my mind. Maybe my heart is lying to me.
Maybe it's telling me to chase her, but my mind tells
me not to. That it won't work out, but my heart wants
to take that chance. She's probably talking with some
other guy right now, sharing "haha's" and exchanging
emojis. They're meeting up for drinks later and kissing
in the basement of a college house. It's complicated.
I've got to give it a shot otherwise I'll hate myself
forever. Looking at you makes me want to risk it all
even if it means hearting my own heart. And if
immense pain now wards off long term pain, then it'd
be foolish for me not to take that shot even if it's
straight to the chest.

Sunday Morning

I wish you could see the beauty that comes with each morning. When I wake before you, it is my favorite part of the day. Sometimes you'll fidget and other times your feet will sneak over to my side of the bed. (Gosh, your feet are cold sometimes.) I get to see you unfiltered. I see you organically. I see you before the make up gets put on. You lay in an oversized t-shirt and smile as you sleep. That's not your favorite smile of mine though, but it's in the top two. No, the smile that is my favorite is when you're doing something you love and your tongue curls over your teeth as you smile. This is a happiness I wish I could bottle up and save for days when are apart or when a simple "miss you" text doesn't do the trick. I try to slip away to go and make chocolate chip pancakes on this Sunday before church. Your hands wrap around my arm and pull me back in and force me to stay a little longer. (Have you been awake this whole time?) You know the powers that you have over me and I don't mind the consequences.

Home Team

I found a spot in the bleachers. I'll be your biggest
fan. Wet marker will grace large pieces of paper each
and every day in the form of notes, kisses, back rubs,
and funny faces. While you may be the only one to
see the big sign on most days, I want you to know
that I am here for you. I'll support "our team" when
we are on a winning streak (You got that new job, we
bought our first house, we won a vacation to the
West Coast, etc.). That doesn't mean I won't support
you when times are tough and nobody believes in us
(Distance separates us for weeks because of work,
bills pile high, our pregnancy tests keep coming back
negative). There are no bandwagoners on this team of
ours. We have been supporting each other ever since,
"do you want to go to the game with me?" With you,
I'm a season ticket holder and I'll never stop being a
fan of us.

To Know Us

I want to know you. I want to see you at your best and when you're at your worst. I want time to bear no weight when we are together. Let the bed go unmade for a couple of days because we were too busy camping in the living room. Let the leftovers be eagerly awaiting our arrival in the fridge for when we both get home from work and don't feel like cooking. Let the stress fall out of our lives like a water balloon dropped from the top floor of our apartment building. (We probably should've apologized to that guy.) Let our future not be determined by what others say about us, but how we feel when we are together and when we are apart. I don't want to smother you like that bad guy in the film we watched last week, but I don't want to not let you know that you are loved. I want to get to know you. I want to get to know us.

My Thoughts

My thoughts are for you. You awake my soul with the jolt that your kisses bring. Sometimes they are unexpected like a surprise birthday party and other times they seem almost scheduled out like a meeting on my calendar. You aren't keeping me alive, but you make me feel alive. I feel young when I'm in your presence. I feel like a kid with his best friend with an afternoon to kill at a water park on the hottest day of summer. Some would probably say our relationship is unhealthy. (No, we don't need to see each other every waking moment, but literally unhealthy. Have you seen the amount of pizza, beer and ice cream we go through? I'm all for movie nights, but damn! We may need to tone it down a bit.) My thoughts are for you in the manner when I hear that song on the radio, it brings me back to a memory of us or it reminds me of you. My thoughts are for you when I see you need extra sleep in the morning because you've been working tirelessly lately. My thoughts are for you when I am walking back to my car and see the night sky. I can't wait to rush home and take it all in with you from the front porch. My thoughts are with you and they always will be...that is unless you watch an episode of "our show" without me.

Unforgettable

Unforgettable. She's like that song stuck in your head that you can't get enough of. She's like your favorite TV show to watch. Each day you spend with her you are on the edge of your seat and are unsure where your adventure with her will take you next. She's like that favorite meal that your mom cooks. The smell of her perfume wafts through the air, makes it's way into your nostrils and suddenly, you're in heaven. It sticks on your t-shirts that you are reluctant to wash and on the blanket you used last week for a movie night with her. She's a little hot to touch sometimes, but you don't mind the burn every now and then. She's unforgettable with the love that she shows you. Don't make an unforgettable woman become a nightmare. Love her with all you've got.

A Girl Worth Fighting For

We tend to search for love in all of the wrong places. We go places that are uncomfortable for many us in hopes our true love will walk through the door at 2am. We aren't going to places we like to go to in order to search for our life companion. We want to have all of these things in common with people and we go through this checklist in our minds. "Oh, they don't like my favorite band? That's a no." And we cross them off of our list mentally. We continually do this because we think there are endless options out there for us, which there are to a certain extent, but we fantasize about there being "the one." We change up the thing about the other person that doesn't make them "perfect" and we move on to the next person. This cycle can be scary and often leaves us wondering, what if I end up alone? Hold up, you're young. Don't lose sleep over ending up alone just yet. Go out and do the things you love to do and go to the places that you like to hang out at and eventually there will come a time when everything will fall into place. Just be sure to speak up when that opportunity asks if the seat next to you is taken.

Hand In Hand

I want to hold your hand. I want to have your hand in marriage. I want to keep them warm when your hands are cold on a walk when almost all of the leaves have fallen. I want to take you by the hand and spin you around on the dance floor whether we know what we are doing or not. (We probably should've signed up for a class. Do you think they'll notice?) I want your hand in mine whenever sickness finds you. I want to be by your side. When our child is on the way and you need to find strength, I want to hold your hand and cheer on my warrior of a wife. I want to love you out loud. My hands may be rough and a little withered, but the beauty in yours covers the blemishes that no one but you can see.

Tomboy

She's a pair of jeans over a sun dress. She's a ball cap
and a beer type of woman. She's a little rock and roll.
She's a cannon baller instead of easing into the pool.
She's the partner that will run the pool table with you
on Friday night. She's a bags partner that you can
count on at your friend's BBQ. She wears her heart
on her sleeve and isn't afraid to speak her mind. Don't
think that just because she has a little edge to her that
she isn't beautiful. She's still a heartbreaker whether
she's in shoes or high heels. She knows what to do to
make you crumble at the sight of her. Loving her is
like closing your eyes and pointing to a spot on a map
and heading there. She's an adventure with everyday.

21st Century Love

She's more than just a bubble on your phone screen.
She's not someone to just text when you're lonely at
2am. She's not a booty call. She's not someone you
love one night and then leave alone. She's a woman.
She deserves your thoughtfulness. Little notes left on
the counter and nights spent learning how to cook
her favorite meal. She deserves your honesty. Your
face to face honesty no matter how hard it is to utter
the words out of your mouth. She deserves your
respect. Be her best friend, but don't smother her.
Give her space and trust her when she's away from
you. We can't throw around people's hearts like it
means nothing. It's becoming too easy to do these
days. Live passionately. Love passionately. Pray
passionately. She deserves that.

To Learn Her

You'll come to learn that she's the type of woman that finds happiness in the little things. She likes to lick the frosting out of the inside of Oreos. She enjoys a cold iced tea out on the front porch on a hot summer day. She is a stealer of the covers and welcomes the title whole heartedly. She will mess with the radio in your car and will most likely change it to the music her and her mom used to jam to. You'll come to find that she's so simple and sweet. She'll spend her days off of work on horseback and a few nights a week out with friends. She finds her comfort in a warm bath with bubbles and a Nicholas Sparks book. You'll come to find that she will lead you closer to the cross. You can bet your bottom dollar that grace will be said before meals and you will be in a church pew come Sunday morning. She won't force you to do it, but you see that she glows even more when you care about your faith. You're going to learn new things about her each and everyday. The more you learn about her, the more you will fall in love with her.

Just For A Moment

Just for a moment, let's be still. Let's pretend it's only you and I. Let's cast all of our fears, our worries and doubts off to the side. I'll grab a blanket and meet you in the back yard. We will gaze up at the stars in the sky until we can't handle the mosquitoes anymore. Just for a moment, let's be still. Let's jump into puddles like we are kids again. Let's kick off our shoes and get our feet dirty. We will slip and slide all over the place and soak up the rain together. Just for a moment, let's be still. Let's pop a couple bags of popcorn and build a blanket fort. We will watch homemade videos and old Disney VHS tapes. We will sing the songs word for word and there will be no one to judge us. Just for a moment, let's be still. Let's grab a burger and a shake and pretend we traveled back in time to the 50s. We will dance in our socks to music our grandparents used to listen to. Just for a moment, let it be you and I.

Rainy Day Thoughts

I'll love you when you're close to me. I'll love you when you're thousands of miles away. I'll love when you show up early and when you show up late. I'll love you when steal all of the covers and leave me shivering with a small sheet. I'll love you in the morning when you sneak up behind me while I'm making breakfast and you become my human backpack. I'll love you in the night when you leave something out and I trip over it on the way to the bathroom. I will love you on the days when your smile won't leave your face and on the days when you need your space. When the sunshine warms our skin as we walk along the street while sharing headphones. When the rain falls and we can't decide on a movie to watch. When you're sick in bed and fill the floor with snot filled Kleenex. When the bills come and we need to cut back our spending. When the tears fall because of my doing or something to do with your friends or work. This love will not be easy and this love will not be perfect, but I will try my best because you're worth it.

Christmas Everyday

Give. Give her your time. Give her one of your favorite sweatshirts to wear. Give her a piggyback ride down the hall. Give her your attention. Turn off your phone more often when you're with her. Give her laughter. Give her tears of joy and make her sides ache. Give her compliments. Let her know when she takes your breath away. Let her know that she is loved. Give her a hand. Help her whether she asks for your help or not. Be there for her. Give her your ear. Listen to her and talk through things with her. You don't have to spend a lot of money on gifts, just give her your presence.

Anywhere With You

Let's take a ride together. We can go up in the mountains or down to the beach. We can go out West and drive along the coast or travel out East and be tourists in the Big Apple. We can take pictures next to unique little shops that we stop at. We can try new foods and share from each other's plates. (Hands off my fries though.) We can spend the night in a sketchy hotel and tell ghost stories with a flashlight under our chins. As cliché as this is going to sound, it doesn't matter where I'm at, as long as you're by my side. You're my shotgun rider. My sing along to the radio partner. My person that feeds me like I'm a zoo animal because I need two hands on the wheel. The person I look over to who is asleep in the passenger seat and my heart feels full. "How'd I get so lucky?" Let's take a ride together.

A Word Not Thrown Around Too Often

The commitment is what she is looking for. The "I'm not leaving until we fix this and work it out," type of man. She's had her fair share of boys who walk in and out of her life. The boys who are afraid of putting the time in when things get difficult. The boys who are afraid to hold her hand, kiss her cheek, take a walk with, help her finish something for work, etc. She's not hoping and praying for Prince Charming, but she's tired. Tired of being an after thought and not a priority. Tired of coming home for the holidays and her family asking her how come she hasn't found anyone yet. Tired of the tears shed because a boy broke her heart and the empty box of wine that rests on the counter waiting to be thrown out. She's worth every kiss, every meal, every date night, every moonlight adventure on the town, every day spent in bed, every trip to the grocery store because she is craving strawberries at 1am and every lump in your throat when you are trying to work things out together. You see the love the old couples have? You can have that.

Anyway You Want It

We all want that love that is like lightning in a bottle. That kind of love that makes your momma smile and all of your exes jealous. We want the long nights in the back of a pickup truck with the radio on while wrapped up in a blanket together. We want the stuck at the top of the Ferris Wheel on a warm summer night. We want the hand in hand walking down the street, "hey, look at those two love birds." We want the "love you's" the "drive safe's" and the long kisses goodbye. We all want to be the definition of a perfect couple. What happens behind the Instagram and Facebook posts? What happens when you're not in the public eye? Is the love still there? Is the commitment to one another still there? There's no such thing as a perfect relationship. Social media gives us a chance to look ideal or perfect, but what about the messiness of love? What about the tears, the disagreements and the nights spent sleeping in different rooms? That's when you find out if you truly love one another. If you can get through the messiness together and embrace it, then you are on the right track. We all want the 80s film type of love, but are we willing to be there for one another when the world feels like it's crashing down?

Take Me By The Hand

Let's get a little bit crazy together. Let's take a chance on our hopes and dreams. You've got something special and I can't let you walk away and leave. Let's do a little bit of traveling together. Let's spend our money on memories, fast food and gasoline. You've got something special and there's a whole world for us to see. Let's have a little wedding together. We'll invite our close friends and our family. Let's stuff our faces with a big piece of cake and dance the night away. You've got something special and I want you to marry me. Let's raise a little family together. A girl named Emily and a boy named Chase. We'll build a house in the country and raise our children to love the land, love people and love God. You've got something special and you'll make a wonderful mother. Let's grow a little bit older together. We'll have no regrets when we look back on the photographs and memories. You've got something special and I will follow your lead.

Dalton Hessel

The Way I Need You

The way I need you. These feelings don't come and go like they did before. They wash over me and stay constant like the steady flow of a river. They bathe in my heart and don't want to ever leave even after they've been called home for supper. I need you the way a farmer needs rain to fall on his crops during a dry summer. A good long soak to fill me up again. I need you like a little kid needs a fresh dusting of snow on Christmas morning. You bring joy to my heart and a smile to my face. I peel back the covers and everyday is a gift with you for you are so beautiful, yet you are so unaware of it.

Pray For Her

Pray for her. You don't think you're ever going to find her. You're starting to believe that "nice guys finish last". Don't abandon the values and morals that you were raised on. Be you. Be the same guy who opens doors, gives a firm handshake, says his "please" and "thank yous", etc. We often get so caught up in our loneliness that we feel this enormous pressure of finding a woman. We think we have to change ourselves because we are tired of being lonely or we feel empty. Often times we are steered in the wrong direction due to lustful desires or whatever the situation may be. Seek the Lord first and then pray for her. Pray that she finds strength on those days that bring her to tears. Pray that she finds happiness with each and everyday. Pray that she drives home safe at night. Pray that she is having fun with her friends. Pray that she finds time to spend with her family and keep them close to her heart even though she may be far from them at work or at college. You may not know her yet, but she's out there. This is not wasted prayer. Pray for timing and find comfort in knowing that she's probably praying for you too.

Looks Like We Made It

I imagine all of these thrown out mixtapes and mix CD's made. A pile of lost love and lost friendships, but then I imagine all of the ones that made it. The ones still in the tape deck or the CD slot. The ones that lift their spirits and bring a smile to their face. Make them feel in love and feel loved. The songs they know all of the words to by heart. It's much better to think about those mixtapes than the ones sitting in the middle of the road waiting to get run over by another car.

Unexpected Beauty

Maybe it's the way that she hops out of bed in the morning. Maybe it's the way she blares Carrie Underwood as she gets ready with the hair dryer on full blast. I swear she forgets that I'm asleep sometimes...or at least pretending to be. Maybe it's the soft touch of her hands as she draws pictures on my back while we watch TV at night. I keep guessing what she's drawing, but I'm wrong 99.9% of the time. I got it right once. It was a tree. She gave me a kiss on the cheek for that. Maybe it's the way she rips up her pancakes before she drowns them in syrup. Maybe it's the pile of clothes she leaves on the floor. She hides in them from time to time and scares me when I get home. A friend of mine asked me why I like her so much. I told him it's because of all of the things that she does that she doesn't notice that she's doing. She knows what she's doing when she puts her hand on my knee. She knows what she's doing when she falls asleep on my shoulder as we lay in the back of my truck at the drive in. She knows what she's doing when she grabs my hands and blows into them to warm them up. She doesn't know what she's doing when she's practicing the dance moves to "Thriller" in the mirror and she accidentally left the door cracked so I could see her. That's what is so special about her. It's finding the beauty in the unexpected, the miscalculated and loving everything about it.

Her Wall of Fame

The photographs scattered all over her bedroom wall tell you a great deal about who is important in her life. Each picture hung with care and thoughtfulness by a clothes pin. They've captured moments important to her. The weekends spent out on the lake with friends, road trips to far away places, family vacations, pictures with teammates, graduation, and pictures of her pets. You could be up on that wall soon. But your residency may be short if you don't treat her right. Treat her like a lady. Respect the hell out of her. Make an effort, show her you care consistently, not just when it's convenient. Don't give her a reason to take down your photo and toss it into the fire.

Waiting For A Girl Like You

In the back right corner of my sock drawer there sits a condom. Wrapped in blue packaging with white lettering streaming across it. I hope when I eventually use it, I don't use it with the wrong woman. I hope I don't use it with a woman who will leave in the morning and I will never see again. I hope I don't use it on wasted love that I don't see going anywhere. I hope I don't use it on a woman whose laugh I don't smile because of. On a face that I can't imagine waking up to everyday. On a woman who's hair I can't imagine finding in my ball cap. On a woman who I can't rush home to and tell how my day went and hear about hers as well. On a woman who doesn't bring out the best in me. I fear that if I use it with the wrong woman, the gift of it is gone. It is no longer special. No longer meaningful and carries little to no weight with it. It is just a word thrown around in conversations with the guys at a friend's house. It's not intimate, it's just another thing to talk about like the score of the game from last Sunday. It can't be like that. It has to mean more than that to me and to her. Because of it doesn't. If it doesn't mean a future together, a lifetime of morning breath, nights spent in bleachers, road trips to God knows where, Chinese food eaten in bed, walks in the woods, and nights spent figuring out how the hell we are going to pay the bills, then I don't want any part of that. It can stay in the sock drawer forever for all I care.

Believe In A Thing Called Love

The way she looks at you tells you all you need to know. When she's with you, her eyes sparkle and there's hope in them. The size of her smile says a lot as well. She believes in you. You should believe in her as well. Believe that you'll be the one to hold her hand. Believe that you'll be the one that eats supper at the table with her. Believe that you'll be the one sitting next to her in church in Sunday's and making faces at the little kids in the row ahead of you. Believe that you'll be the one picking her up at the airport after she went to visit her college roommate. Believe that happiness will be found on the days where you do absolutely nothing, but lie on the couch and watch movies while eating whatever you can find in the cupboards. She believes in you like the she believes that the sun will rise each morning. Why shouldn't you do the same?

Mr. Consistency

It's not only on display just for the big days. Her birthday, Valentine's Day, your anniversary, etc. It's all those little days in between. The days when she feels like she could be a member of *The Walking Dead* with how sick she feels. It's making her hot soup, rubbing her feet, and a quick "let me run a hot bath for ya". It's the days when she comes home from work after having a horrible day. It's the days when you don't tell her where you're going, but she hops in the truck anyway and goes along for the adventure. It's checking in with a quick call just to see how her day is going. It's listening to her and being there for her even if you had the best day of your life and not telling her about it It's the long talks at night, curled up in bed, about your theories as to why they killed off a certain character in the tv show you watch together. It's the, "she woke up late but you're driving her to work in your pajamas" kind of day. It's consistent. It's consistent love. It appears on good days and bad days. It is on display for everyone to see, but is also very intimate. Don't let the movies fool you, consistent love is the kind of love that you need to show her...but yeah, doing crazy romantic things to show her how much you care for her is pretty awesome, too.

Wild Child

She's the cup of coffee spilt on the front of your shirt: hot and unexpected. She surprised you. She made her way into your life like an accidental curly fry. She's the reason you can't fall asleep at night. No, not because you are dreaming about her, but because she made you watch that scary movie with her and certain things can't be unseen. You're brain is going to tell you to run away as fast as you can, but you've got to listen to your heart on this one. She's going to pull you out on the dance floor. She's going to drive fast and take corners hard. She's going to make mistakes. She's going to break your favorite glass one night. (Yes, that intramural championship one.) She's going to burn a meal or two. But you're going to make mistakes, too. You're going to forget to pick her up one afternoon and she's going to walk home in the rain. Don't worry, she'll forgive you for that one, but not before pouncing on you and getting you all wet once she comes through the front door. You're going to disagree on things and that's ok. What you can't do is let those mistakes, disagreements, and differences tear you apart. She may be a little too rock n' roll for your taste, but don't be too set in your ways to not listen to the music she has to offer.

Set The Hook

She's named after her grandmother. She's sarcastic like her father. She is a free spirit who could care less what people think about her. She isn't reckless, but that's not saying she won't jump off the rocks at the old mining shaft to go for swim. She isn't like any girl you'll meet at the bar and never call back. She's a life changer. She's the kind of girl that knocks on your front door at 6am on a Saturday and wants to go on an adventure. She's the kind of girl that throws the first snowball to start a snowball fight on your driveway. She's the kind of girl who will wake you up by tickling you with her hair. She isn't ashamed to wear her heart on her sleeve. She laughs at the little things, like the funny faces you make through the car window as you pick her up from work. She makes you laugh hard, the kind that takes your breath away and makes your sides hurt. Her love for you will shine brighter every day that passes. She'll leave notes for you on the kitchen counter with scribbled directions on where to find her because she can't stand another night in the house. She'll take you blackberry picking and have you spending the afternoon being the official taste tester. A job title you proudly accept. She casts her own line in the water and whether you take the bait and pursue her is up to you. But if you take the bait, she's got you hook, line, and sinker.

Thinking Out Loud

I fell in love with you because of the little things you never knew you were doing. The way you smile at and interact with complete strangers: the waitress, the kid in the shopping kart, the old man sipping his coffee on the street bench. The way you bite on your lower lip when you're really concentrating on something you're reading. The way you look up at the street lights and have this optimistic look in your eyes. Your handwriting on the notes you write for class and even the hearts that you put on your "I"s. You say it's cliché, but you do it anyways. The way you tie up your hair when it's time for you to "get down to business." The excitement in your voice whenever you are telling a story. The way you get antsy in your seat when the game is on and find yourself more excited than me when we score. It's all of these little things and more that make me fall in love with you more each day.

Stay Single Until...

Stay single until you meet the girl that isn't afraid to tease you. That walks to the beat of her own drum. That says whatever is on her mind.

Stay single until you meet the girl that sings at the top of her lungs in the shower. Disney classics, boy bands, show tunes, etc. She isn't ashamed about it.

Stay single until you meet the girl that unapologetically steals your flannels and sweatshirts and isn't afraid to get them dirty. She longs for adventure and takes you along for the ride.

Stay single until you meet the girl that calls you out when you're doing something wrong. She's honest with you whether you want to hear it or not. The one that makes you work a little harder to impress her because she isn't like any other girl you've met before. Stay single until you meet the girl that makes you jump in the water with her on a hot and sticky, starry summer night. Stay single until you meet the girl that you gush to your friends about and can't wait to see again. The one you write letters to in the middle of the day because something reminded you of her.

Stay single until you meet the girl that you can tell your secrets to (yes, even the ones involving that year you were obsessed with High School Musical.) The girl that makes you nervous before your first date. The girl that makes you want to take your time in a society that tells you the opposite. The one you look at and see a good mother in. The one that you can raise a family with. Stay single until you meet the girl that makes you say, "finally." She's worth the wait.

Our Fridge

Who knew we could fit so much on this thing? Magnets hold up pictures, save the dates and grocery lists like Rafiki holding up Simba for the first time. (Good call by picking up those Disney magnets at that garage sale.) Do you remember the night these photos were taken? We must have spent hours in that photo booth. I'm not exactly sure if it was the beer talking or if we were just that creative that night, but they still make me laugh out loud. Why do we still have this Christmas card on the fridge? Oh, it's our first Christmas card together? My bad honey. Look at how small Lambeau (our dog) was! That reminds me, we need to take him to get shots soon. What's that you have there? That gift certificate expires soon I think. Yep, it does. Never mind. Let's make a pizza and catch up on Game of Thrones.

The Reason I Can't Stop Looking At My Phone

The funny face photos you send me fill my phone. I look at them when I am having a bad day at work or when I just need to put myself in a better mood. There's something about your carefree faces. The one with your eyes crossed and your tongue out is my favorite. No, wait. My favorite one is the one where you look like a chipmunk with your cheeks puffed out as if they'll burst at a moments notice. There's so much beauty in your candidness. I'm not sure if you feel the same way about the photos I send you, but hey, they've got to be better than any unsolicited photos of a dude's junk that you've received over the years.

The Winning Ticket

I play the lottery everyday. Each day is a chance to win big. I have yet to get the right combination, but I pray that it's coming soon. It'll happen eventually, right? With each day the sun rises and sets, but I'm not a winner and crinkle up my ticket. I throw it into the trash and hope for a better tomorrow. What would I do with my winnings? That's a simple question. I'd put a ring on her finger fast, but not too fast. Sometimes you've got to double-check your numbers to make sure you didn't make a mistake. After double-checking, I would buy a house maybe out in the country. I'd like to think I am a simple man, but my winnings may have other plans and you know what? That's fine by me.

Is This Thing On?

Speak up. Stop pretending that she's going to be the one to break the silence. As you silence yourself each day, you are giving someone else a chance to build that connection. You can't be angry at the guy that talked to her instead. He fought off the lions in his heart telling him to be quiet. Jealousy is formed by chances that weren't taken.

From Veteran To Rookie

"That was a routine fly ball", "That was a routine double play", "That was a routine dunk". Routine is a word that is often thrown around in the sports world. Saying something is "routine" means that it is expected. It's what you would predict to happen. But, do we notice how routine our lives can be sometimes? You may wake up at the same time everyday, eat the same brand of cereal, drink out of the same coffee cup, see the same people on your way to work, etc. Days start feeling like you're in the movie *Groundhog Day*. While many of us may enjoy the predictability of life, I encourage you to break the routine. Bike to work instead of drive, eat at a different place, try listening to new music, etc. Whatever you have to do. Life is too short to not be living. Make extraordinary plays.

Hot 'N Cold

There are going to be moments when you believe in it like a five-year-old believes in Santa. You'll trust in it, your heart will be full of it, you'll talk about it constantly, you'll sing about it, dance about it, celebrate it, and write about it. You'll take it places with you. It'll fill your phone with pictures and cover your office desk with gifts. You don't think it'll ever go away. Then there are going to be moments where you swear it off forever. You'll turn away from it, you won't want to hear about it, see it, or talk about it. You'll destroy it like a fire consuming a house. You'll want nothing to do with it. Even when you think it'll never happen to you again or you'll never believe in it, your heart will wake up from its cold winter hibernation.

Hold Your Breath

This feels like we're falling in love. The last breath of summer is being taken and I hope it holds onto it until it's blue in the face. I'm not ready to pack up my Jeep and head back to the university. Leaves, stay on the trees. If you fall, it will kill me. Sun, stay in the sky for as long as you can. Tourists, don't pack up your things just yet. Stay. Maybe we will text or call. Maybe we will Skype. Maybe we will see each other on weekends. I don't want to think about all of the maybes. I want to think about the here and now. Your face buried in my chest as we hug for what feels like the last time. Leaves, stop falling! No, no, sun stay in the sky! Moon, what are you doing? Tourists, stop packing up! Stop! Stop! Stop! Can't you hear me? Summer lets out its final breath and I'm left with a cold breeze, longing for a sweatshirt and a new heart.

The Bucket

You fill me up like raindrops in the plastic bucket next to the porch. Even when I appear filled, you find a way to fill me up even more and I begin to pour out of the sides. I pray for the water to never run dry. I pray that no drought may strike and everything evaporates. I pray that I am not left with cottonmouth. If a dry spell occurs, I will seek a rainmaker or do a rain dance, or whatever I have got to do to keep the stream alive. Your love is worth drowning for and I cast the lifejacket aside like a careless fisherman.

Maxing Out The Speakers

I want to love you out loud. Trust that I will love you
more than just on special days. Trust that I will love
you more than posting a picture of us every now and
then. Trust that I will chase you every day. Have you
ever maxed out the speakers in your car? Yeah, that
kind of loud. Put me on a rooftop with a megaphone
kind of love. "Tonight we are going out on the town.
Be at your place in five," kind of love. While I am
busy screaming at the top of my lungs, I hope your
voice isn't a whisper. I don't want to rush into things
like I'm a sixteen year old buying my first car. (Not
that I'm comparing you to a car.) I just want to take
my time with you because you're the song stuck in my
head that I can't stop singing.

Crash Test Dummy

Maybe it's not as crazy as it sounds—the two of us together. They say that if you do same thing repeatedly and expect different results, you're crazy. With you, it feels like I'm driving my car into the wall at 60mph and expect to walk away without a scratch. The shards of broken glass cut me and I'm left with bumps and bruises. But you'll see me do the same thing the next day. I put the car into drive again without hesitation. My knuckles turn white as I grip the steering wheel with both hands, pretending like I have any control.

Made With Love

My mom used to bake cookies all of the time. She'd devote her day to laundry, sweeping the floors, vacuuming, and baking cookies. She'd place the cookies on the cooling rack so delicately it was like she was performing surgery. The next day, she'd pile them all into an old ice cream bucket, along with a slice of bread so that they'd stay fresh. "Made with love," is what the sticky note on top of the bucket would typically say. I often wondered what that meant. *Made with love?* But it's starting to make sense the more and more I cook with you. Made with love means embracing the mistakes. Not every meal is going to turn out perfectly. Gordon Ramsey would toss me off his show in a heartbeat. There may be burn marks or maybe you added a little too much salt, but for the most part everything tastes like it should. Made with love means not being afraid to get a little messy. Put a little flour on your face and swing your hips to the radio. You lick the batter off of the spoon and you reluctantly agree to let me have whatever is left in the bowl. You give me such a sad look when you hand it over like I just told you Christmas was cancelled. Made with love takes time. It takes patience. As badly as you want to eat, you've got to let it cook.

Hands On The Clock

You keep me waiting. I check my watch constantly, but not like I am going to be late for something. We will get there when we get there. You keep me waiting for your reply. I feel the jolt in my pocket and everything else in the moment gets put on the backburner. I realize how dangerous this is, but like a child reaching into the cookie jar before dinner, I can't help myself. You keep me waiting for you as I let out the words from my mouth that I can't take back no matter how afraid I am to let them out. "W- would you want to go on a date?" I don't know if you're pausing for dramatic effect with your response, but you finally say, "yes," and I can breathe again. You keep me waiting at the front door as you finish getting ready. You call me a nerd for bringing you flowers, but you smile as you smell them. You keep me waiting as I stand next to my best friends as you and your father walk down the isle. (Sorry for not getting the doves to fly in front of you. They're overrated anyways.) You keep me waiting as you read whether or not we will become a family of three. With no music playing, we dance around the living room like two kids hyped up on way too much sugar. You keep me waiting for you to come home from work so we can talk about our days. You vent to me. You talk in different voices that go along with your co-workers. I try to conceal my laughter by covering my face with my hand, but it's no use. You catch me and I know I'll pay for it later. You keep me waiting as I lay in the hospital bed. You grab my hand tightly and kiss it as I take my final breath. I hopefully make it to heaven, but judging by the length of the "to do list" that still rests on the counter, I feel as though I will wind up in a place much warmer. You keep me waiting in the land of milk and honey, but don't worry, take your time.

The Big Apple

You give me that New York City feeling no matter where I am; the feeling that Sinatra sang about. You make me feel like a tourist in the heart of the city. I never want to stop taking photos. You make me feel like a somebody on a street that is shoulder to shoulder with people. Everybody else is scrambling to get on their subway, to throw themselves into a cab, or is running down the streets because they are late. With you there's no rush. We hold open doors for people for what feels like hours because we are "Midwest nice" and can't help ourselves. We stop in stores and check out how the other half lives. We try on clothes that have way too many commas on their price tags. I might as well throw my watch away when I am with you. People say that New York is the city that never sleeps and now I see why. How could anyone sleep when such beauty is before them?

You Drive

I love it when you drive instead of me. No, it's not just because I like saving money on gas, but I love to watch you drive. One moment you'll be happy while jamming to John Mayer and the next you'll think I switched the CD to heavy metal as you ream out a driver that cut you off. You don't appreciate it that I laugh at you when you're angry. You'll have to forgive me with a playful punch to the shoulder. You're so cute when you're mad. Your nose scrunches up and your hands grip the steering wheel tightly. You let out a few deep breaths like a mother who is stuck in traffic with a backseat full of noisy children. We ultimately get the radio back to Mayer and all is well with the world. "Quit laughing at me," you say. But it's hard not to smile with the view I have from the passenger seat...until you take a corner too hard that is. My face gets pressed against the window and snozzberries begin tasting like snozzberries.

4 FUTURE LOVE STORIES

Piña Coladas

His shoelaces began to unravel as he propelled himself further down the street. Rain leaving marks on his sweatshirt like his dog's drool that often fell on his shoulder. His car was still five blocks away. "Walk," he mumbled to himself sarcastically as he looked up at the sky. "You need the exercise." He could only chuckle to himself now. Using the penny saver newspaper to cover his hair, he began to jog. The coins and keys jiggling in his pocket made him sound like a one-man band. Geniuses passed him with their umbrellas and smiled at him. The newspaper began to soak through and crumble in his hands. "Only a block or two left," he said to himself. He came to terms that he was already soaked, so he finally bent over to tie his shoes. The rain over head suddenly ceased, but continued to fall around him. "God? Is that you?" he thought to himself. "You can stand under my umbrella, 'ella, 'ella, eh, eh..." the woman, (I mean, angel) standing next to him said. He looked up and smiled. Her hood was propped up, but her brown hair was protruding out of the sides. Her smile was wide like she just ate the last cookie in the jar without telling anybody. "Yes, it is I, the brilliant mind who forgot an umbrella," he said. "Don't beat yourself up," she replied. "I was young once too." She couldn't have been any older than he, but she had a certain wit about her that he always admired in a woman. Blindsided by the rain as he was, he was happy to have left his brain and his umbrella on the hook at home.

Sundays Are For Lovers

A blanket, a couple of pillows, some snacks and pocket full of cash is all he packed. "That's it?" she said as they stood in the drive way. "What?" he replied. "You said you wanted to be more spontaneous." She shook her head and smiled. She knew he was trying to impress her and take her on an adventure, but all she wanted to do today was read out on the porch. "Come on! I've got a whole day trip planned for us!" She folded her arms and cocked her head to the side. "I don't know," she said. "I've got a lot to get done around the house today." He could tell she was a little hesitant, but he knew she needed a day away from the house. She needed a day of laughter, random pictures, and a jam session with the radio. "I didn't want to have to do this, but you leave me with no choice," he said. He playfully picked her up and was able to get her into the passenger seat all the while they were laughing. "This is your captain speaking," he said as he pretended to talk into a microphone. "Where we are headed, I am the only one who knows. So sit back, put your feet out of the window and get ready for an adventure." She shoved the bill of his hat down over his face and kissed him on the cheek.

Basement Love Story

Red solo cups blanketed the floor and puddles of God knows what began to form. Their bodies were slowly (or quickly for some) beginning to fill with alcohol as they danced and conversed over loud rap music society told them was cool. Corners were the home of make out sessions, whether they were welcomed or not. A slight haze appeared through the bright lights that were cast from the DJ booth. He was with friends for a night out after a long week of class. She was there because she needed an excuse to not stay in again and binge watch "Friends" on Netflix. "Who is that?" he shouted to his friend over the music. His hand was extended out like he was trying to guide a lost traveler. "I don't know, but you should go talk to her," his friend replied. He took a long drink of his Old Milwaukee and he began to make his way over to her.

Countless feet were stepped on in the process and numerous drinks were spilt on him. "Shouldn't have worn my favorite shirt," he thought to himself. "Hey, we have biology class together," a face he did not recognize said. He was terrible with names, but even worse when it came to faces at times. He tried to match this stranger's excitement, but his mind and eyes were elsewhere. The music seemed like a whisper now and the stranger's voice sounded like Charlie Brown's teacher's as he stayed focused on her.

Her brown hair was let down and graced the top of her Twins shirt while she sipped on a Mike's Hard Lemonade. He started to laugh as she laughed without ever hearing whatever joke was told. He began to feel butterflies in his stomach (or was it the beer?). "Cool shirt," he said as her friends stopped talking. (Cool shirt? Smooth…). "Thanks," she replied. "Are you a Twins fan, too?" At least she was making an attempt to help this awkward duckling out. For once she was glad she wasn't approached by someone complimenting her on her looks. Both of them were unaware of just how much Trevor's party was going to mean to them someday.

Morning Buzz

The barely ticking wristwatch rests on the nightstand. The open windows carry the weight of dangling dew on their screens. The morning's soft breeze is enough to make the curtains dance in the sunlight. An eager alarm clock ready to jump off of the table is screaming hysterically. He reluctantly rolls over to stop the sound that is piercing his ears. His hand misses the alarm clock a few times, knocking off his phone in the process before finally being able shut off the angry keeper of time. He wipes his face as he feels the bristles of his beard against his hands. The phone still rests on the carpet floor. He knows that if he picks it up that her message will not be waiting for him. Maybe this time it'll be different, he thinks to himself. With eyes closed tightly, he flips over the phone and awaits its verdict as he slowly opens them. "Coffee?" it reads. It was from her. Coffee? Tea? Crumpets? I don't care what we meet over as long as I can see her again, he thought. He threw on his coat, jumped into his Levi's and was out the door. He got to the coffee house first and began to write down all of the things he wanted to say to her. His heart feeling non-existent after he put it on the pages of his notebook and awaited her arrival.

Flowers

She now sits where she once sat. She smiles at him and he smiles back as he plays with her hair. She gives him kisses when he least expects it. He goes to wipe his face, but he thinks it might offend her, so he fights off the urge. They pass billboards and mile markers as the white stripes blur and ease his mind. He begins to think back to when she used to sit in that seat. He pops in a cassette and turns the volume knob to the right. His mind wanders back to the night when he picked her up for their first date. "You clean up well for a farm boy," she said as he helped her up into his '65 Chevy pickup truck. He took her all over town, experiencing it together like they were tourists in their own hometown. The streetlights above their heads created shadows on the cracked sidewalk where they walked together hand in hand. His hands were unsteady and sweaty, but he slowly relaxed when he saw her wipe her hands off on her dress. "Sorry," she said, "just a little nervous." "Would it help if I kissed you?" he replied. He brushed her hair over her ear. "It's worth a shot," she said. He looks at the photo taken on their wedding day every now and then. His heart doesn't race anymore, but he feels calm and finds comfort. "We're here," he said to his whiskered shotgun companion, Bailey. He grabbed the flowers out of the backseat and went to her grave to fall in love all over again.

Taking A Sip

Across the table she sits. Not making much sound, but she came out to eat with him anyways. She needed it whether she knew it or not. "Two cups of coffee, please," he told the waitress. The waitress smiled and left them to be alone. "Everything okay? You don't seem yourself lately," he said to her. She shrugged her shoulders and said, "I don't know." Her voice was almost a whisper acting as though she was still in bed. He had to find out what was eating her up inside. He wanted the old her back. He wanted the adventurous side of her back. The wake me up in the middle of the night to make cookies and watch reruns of "Boy Meets World" kind of girl. The girl that would steal his dress shirts and wear them to bed. The girl that laughed uncontrollably at dinner and occasionally made bubbles with a straw in her milk. "Is it something I did?" He pried. "I'm pregnant," she uttered. The waitress returned and set down their coffees, unaware of how much had changed since her short disappearance.

Ice Cream Dreams

It sat there on the corner of Graham and Jefferson Street for God knows how long. The weather wearing it down year after year. Paint was fading and rust spread like a cancer across the bottom of it. They were going for a drive one Sunday afternoon when she asked him to pull over. "We need to buy this," she said as she patted it on the hood. He squinted at her, not because the sun was shining in his eyes, but more like a baby who tasted a lemon for the first time. "What the heck are we going to do with it?" he asked with his arms folded. He watched her as she examined the interior of this time machine, her face lighting up with every window she looked in. "I don't know," she said, "I was thinking we could make it into an ice cream van." One thing was for sure, he didn't want that creepy ice cream man music radiating through the speakers, but he supported her idea. "We will set up down by the beach. It'll be wonderful!" The joy he saw in her face made him feel like he was being hit by a wave of his favorite love songs all at once. Just to see her smile, he'd do anything.

A Night Out

"I wish I didn't meet you at a bar," she said to him. He had trouble hearing her over the music that the bar had turned up and everyone was screaming along with "Thnks Fr Th Mmrs". He leaned in closer to her. "I wish we met somewhere else, like a coffee shop or something," she shouted. He couldn't help but to think this as well. What was he doing here? He had homework to do, sleep to catch up on and movies he could be watching, but something brought him to the bar that night. He couldn't quite place his finger on it. Was it the stress from school? Had it been a while since he had been out? Yes, and it was nice to see his friends again, he thought. Was he trying to still get over her? Yes, but in a way he was hoping he would see her. He wanted to know she was doing all right. He came back to reality. "I wish we met somewhere else, too," he said to her and he began to make his way through the pile of people and he exited the bar. No, he didn't want to find her anymore, but he knew he wasn't going to find her here.

The Greatest Team

She's his game day girl. The girl that he can scream at the TV with over a touchdown or a blown call. The girl that grew up watching games with her father. She wears her favorite player's jersey like it's a superhero costume. She gets animated when her team scores and is devastated when they lose. They comfort each other after loses with a bowl of ice cream or going outside and throwing eggs at the tree to relieve some stress. They watch every game together. Their bottoms find their way into bleachers and their nightstand is coated with ticket stubs from previous trips to the stadium. They will soon add another player to their roster. The stadiums may get smaller and road trips may only be to near by towns, but their favorite player will be living under their roof.

A Piece Of History

He told her that if he ever won the lottery that they'd buy the place together and fix it up. People told them that it'd be a foolish thing to do. They said it would never bring in a dollar. "They also said that we'd never work out," he told her as they examined the building while on their walk. Ice cream cones accompanied their hands as the heat of the day pounded on their bodies. "What would you want to do with it?" she asked. He took a bite out of his ice cream cone (something she loved to hate) and he said, "I'm not entirely sure, babe." He always imagined turning the building into a little restaurant and a place for artists young and old to share their work. A place where people could come and gather during the endless daze of summer and the fireplace conversations that were carried in with the winter's chill. He looked at the expiring exterior of the building and didn't know if he'd be able to save it in time. He was hopeful though as the two continued their walk. And with every step that he took, it was harder for him to walk away from the building.

The Game

She gives him that 4th quarter game winning drive
type of feeling in his heart. She gives him that bottom
of the 9th, down by one run with the bases loaded
and two outs feeling in his soul. One thing is for
certain, he does not treat her love like a game. This is
one thing he can't play with. Her heart is not to be
used and then thrown out like a ball that got hit over
the fence and lost in the woods. He wakes up like it's
game day everyday with her, waiting for his chance to
prove himself to her. To win her over again and
again.

All Over A Campfire

The two of them were on a road trip. It was their last hurrah as friends until both of them started their new careers. One would work on The East Coast while the other stayed in the Midwest to settle down and start a family soon. The night air was cold enough to make you grab a sweatshirt as they sat around the campfire and passed a bottle of whiskey back and forth. "Do you think she'll say 'yes'?'" the one friend asked the other. "Do you love her?" the friend replied. The young man looked down at the bottle of Jack Daniels while swishing it back and forth, looking for answers in it that he knew he couldn't find. He came back to reality and looked back up at his friend. He set down the bottle and took the ring box out of his jeans pocket. He opened and closed it repeatedly. "I love her. When all seems lost and I cannot seem to handle the storms life throws my way...she is the lighthouse that brings me home. She is the rising sun in the morning that wakes me from my slumber and warms me with her kisses. She is my favorite song to listen to. My favorite dancer to watch. Her body in motion that pulls at my heart like the moon does the tides. 'Do I love her?' It would not feel the same with another. She is intelligent, crafty, comical, brutally

honest, sarcastic, and elegant all thrown into one."
Upon hearing his friend profess his love for this
woman, he gave him a smile. "I'll drink to that," he
said as he motioned for the bottle. His friend already
knew that he loved her, but he just wanted to hear
him talk about her. He loved to see the passion ignite
in his eyes whenever he talked about her. A fire
seemed to burn inside of him. A fire more powerful
than the very one that he was currently being warmed
by.

The Fixer Upper

He looked down at the newspaper clipping that was pinched between his fingers and then back up at the house. It was worse to look at in person. "You sure about this?" He looked over at her. She was wearing a Milwaukee Brewers ball cap with paint spots on it and was sporting blue jeans. "Yes, I'm sure," she replied. "This is my dream home." They opened the door to the house and stepped inside. The hard wood floors creaked as they moved throughout the house. Its wails reminded them of the baby that would soon enter their lives and keep them up at night. The kitchen cabinets were dusty and the doors were slightly crooked. He could tell that she was concerned about this. She always wanted a beautiful kitchen to cook in for big family meals or for when they had friends over. "Don't worry," he said with a smile, "I can fix that." She was instantly reminded of Sam from the book "Holes" and she burst out laughing. A laugh that he had fallen in love with. They moved on to the living room and examined the fireplace. He imagined stoking a fire and leaving his wet clothes out to dry for the night. She imagined a place for stories told with children on her lap as the snow fell outside around Christmas time. They worked their way up to the master bedroom and bathroom. The bathtub was an old claw foot tub that was just big enough to fit the two of them, they thought. "You know you're going to have to run a bath for me at least once a week, right?" He smiled and didn't mind the thought of it at all. Long days of painting walls and rooms with an old paint splattered boombox were in their near future. They were certain more paint would end up on them instead of the walls. Pockets were soon to be filled with nails and screws. Sweat would be sure to find its way into their shirts and drip from their foreheads. They welcome the challenge like the smallest kid on the playground taking on the school bully. The house was simply a house before they came, but when they left to go and make an offer, it felt more and more like home. It was their "grow old together" home.

Kitchen Counter Conversations

"Tell me that we'll always work it out," she said as she sat on kitchen counter. "Of course," he replied, "I love you." He dropped the dishes that he was doing and pulled her close to him. "No matter what?" she asked and she tilted her head to the side. "No matter what," he replied and kissed her on the forehead. The sun was beginning to set and it cast a radiant light through the window and onto her face. "You're my forever girl. I'm going to be there for you when the house is a mess and your parents are on their way over. I'm going to be there for you when you burn dinner. I'm going to be there when we argue about whose turn it is to take out the trash," he slid her closer to him. "When the tears and pain strike you, I will hold you close and rock you. I will take your pain and try the best I can to make it my own as well. We are in this together," he looked into her brown eyes, "no matter what."

Pray That It's Raining

They awoke in the morning to sounds of thunder and rain tapping on the ground outside of their window. He rolled over to face her and she was already looking at him. Those blue eyes of her analyzing his chiseled face and the scripture tattoo written on his chest. It was still early in the morning, and with morning breath and all, she leaned over and gave him a kiss. "What should we do today?" she whispered. He flipped over onto his stomach and opened up the bedroom window. He loved the smell of rain. "I could lay here all day with you," he replied. She looked at him and exposed a beautiful smile as she now flipped over on her stomach to take in the storm with him. "I'd like that," she said. They spent the whole day in bed telling stories from their childhood and laughing while in each other's arms. They made love a time or two as the hands on the clock seemed to stand still when they were together. He read to her as she placed her head on his chest, the tattoo acting as a beacon for her. One of them would occasionally sneak away to grab food for the both of them or to use the bathroom, but they quickly hopped back into the welcoming bed sheets. A rainy day is not only good for the earth, but good for the soul.

Water Tower Promises

"I'll write your name up there someday," he told her as he pointed up towards the water tower. "I want the world to know just how much I love you." She raised an eyebrow and laughed at him. "What?" he said. "It's true." She put her hand on his shoulder like a mother consoling her son after a tough Little League game. "Babe," she said. "You don't need to write it on a water tower. You show everyone how much you love me when you hold my hand. You show everyone how much you love me when we race down the isles at the grocery store in the carts with the wobbly wheels. You show your love for me by making me laugh when all I want to do is cry and when you bring me food when I get angry. As much as I'd love to see 'Carter loves Norah' written on the water tower in spray paint, I already know that you love me." She kissed him on the cheek, smacked him on the butt and ran down the sidewalk for him to chase after her towards the fireworks show.

American Love Story

They met back in high school. He asked her out with a note that he had stuffed through the vents in her locker. He had a crush on her for the longest time and finally got the courage to write down his feelings for her. She wrote a note back that contained only one word, "yes." They spent the rest of their senior year of high school spending night's together. They couldn't remember how many nights they spent around a campfire or how many games of bowling they played during the cold winter months. What they had was simple and special. She was crazy about him and he was crazy about her. After graduation, the hard times came. He went off to boot camp and she worked at her father's grocery store. He would write to her whenever he could, but it was mostly scribblings of, "I love you," and "I'm alive." When they finally reunited, his knees still shook at the sight of her and her blue eyes regained their sparkle. He keeps a picture of her with him while he is thousands of miles away. Each glance he takes of the folded up picture reminds him that he's not so far away from home. The sound of fireworks on the 4th of July bring their two hearts together again.

The Search

He doesn't have a sweetheart yet. He knows that love song type of love is out there for him. He knows that's somebody out there to make plans with. Someone out there who he can try to win carnival prizes for and will spend almost every wrinkled dollar he has to try to win that teddy bear. Someone that can keep him in line, but not control him. He wants the type of love that he's got to work for. That old fashioned love. He wants to drop letters off in her mailbox. He wants to sit on the front porch with her and share a glass of sweet tea. He's not looking for a perfect woman, because he himself is not a perfect man. Some of his friends have checklists that women need to meet. All he wants is a woman his mother and sisters will approve of.

Vintage

"Are you going to kiss me or not?" she asked. Her blue eyes looking into his as she smiled. He grinned and leaned in for his first kiss. With one eye open and one eye closed; he kissed her. He didn't want to miss. She kissed him with her eyes closed so tightly and a smirk forming in the corner of her mouth. The lipstick she spent time putting on in the mirror was now an after thought. She didn't care how messed up it got. Her dress ruffled in the cool summer breeze air. His hands shook as they reached to push the hair out of her face and back behind her ear. The romantic comedies he watched with his mother while growing up taught him that. "Those Saturday nights weren't wasted," he thought to himself.

This was the girl he had been praying for. The kind of girl that makes you want to call in sick for work and take a spontaneous trip with. The kind of girl that makes him want to drop off letters in her mailbox and knock on the door and run away. The kind of girl that he could see filling photo albums with.

This was the guy she had been praying for. The kind of guy that makes you want to sit on the top of the roof with at night with a blanket. The kind of guy that you take home to your father and don't have to worry about the two of them not getting along. The kind of guy that will be open and communicate with her.

And to think, it all started with someone needing a pencil in their college class together.

Save The Last Dance

"Just dance with me," he told her. "Dance with me in the kitchen. Dance with me in the middle of the street. Dance with me on the front porch in the middle of a thunderstorm. Dance with me at your friends and my friends' weddings. When you come home from work and your bag is filled with files, papers and is weighing you down. When you can't help it because you love the song that is playing on the radio. When you're excited about our date night. I may not always be there when you're dancing, but save the last dance for me."

Festival

She tapped him on the arm. "I know this is going to sound weird, but can you put me on your shoulders?" she said. "I can't see." He turned around from the conversation with his friends and locked eyes with her. Well, more like sunglasses. She was wearing a faded red t-shirt that hung off to the side of her left shoulder. Jean shorts with a dirt stain on them from when she tried doing a cartwheel in the field on a dare. Her brown hair was still a little wet from the rain earlier in the day. The drink in her hand was sweating from the summer sun shining down on the two of them. The concert and the crowd now seemed like background music and all he noticed was her. "It may cost you a dance or two later," he replied. "Consider it a done deal," she said as she hopped up onto his shoulders with little to no success on the first few attempts. The rest of the night they belted out each song like they knew all of the words (whether they did or not). She spilt her drink a couple of times on him, but he didn't mind. The music may have stopped at the end of the night. The singers had sung their songs. The guitar strings were no longer being plucked. The bass no longer thumped, but the two hearts were continuing their song.

Along For The Ride

She puts fireworks inside of him that would ignite anytime she walked into the room. She wasn't the kind of girl to dip her toes in the water, she would jump right in. He was rather quiet and reserved until he met her. When they met at a friend's game night, she started to work on that outer shell of his. She didn't want to change him, she just wanted him to start living. Nights spent in photo booths that would turn into photos being held up by magnets on their fridge. Days spent walking and window shopping would turn into hilarious fashion shows and weird looks from strangers. There was no such thing as a quiet ride when they were in the car together. Blink-182 and Jimmy Eat World was what most people were introduced to with their singing at stoplights and out on the highway. Meals would turn into who could get the other person to spit out their drink because they couldn't contain their laughter. His parents always told him to not play with matches, but this girl lit a fire that he couldn't contain.

From The Sidelines

They've got that neon kind of love. Late nights spent at concerts, singing and dancing with strangers like it was the last night of their lives. They've got that firework kind of love. The dangerous Roman Candle pointed directly at you as you run with laughter, but a little fear in your chest. They've got that long conversations on the rooftop with a blanket and a bottle of wine kind of love. It's that love people are jealous of. They don't boast about it. They aren't constantly flaunting it, but people recognize that it is real. You see it in the way they look into each other's eyes. The way they converse about big things such as having kids to the small things like why they always open up Starbursts and get the yellow kind. What they've got is special and you can't help but to root for them and hope they make it.

Catch In The Dark ·

She's got an old soul. She's stubborn in many ways,
but that's one of the reasons you can't get enough of
her. She's the kind of woman that will make you fall
flat on your face in love with her, but she's going to
make you work to get her attention. You see, she's
fallen in love too fast before and she knows now that
her heart is not to be played with. She knows what
long nights on the phone with her mother are like.
She's spent nights in stranger's arms to try to feel that
love again. She's not looking for somebody to change
her, but looking for somebody to love. Love whole
heartedly and to join her on her adventures. A partner
in crime that will help her in pranking her co workers
at night. Someone that will join her out on the dance
floor and dance like nobody is watching. Someone to
drive with her as she hangs her feet out of the
window on the way to the beach. Someone who will
stay up late with her eating cheap pizzas and dunking
Oreos in milk. Loving her is like playing catch in the
dark. You have to trust the process and know that
she'll be there for you and you'll be there for her. All
you've got to do is catch the ball.

Living Out A Country Song

I geeked out the first time I saw her, man. Like, my God, let's raise a dog together. She was eating an ice cream cone and laughing with her little brother when I saw her. Sunglasses, a sun dress, and beautiful her smile was my kryptonite. I probably wasn't her Superman she was looking for, but she made me feel like it. I was on my way back to my truck after picking up some fishing bait from Willie's. I'm not proud of this next moment, but I dropped my bait right in front of her on the sidewalk in order to get a conversation going with her. Worms and dirt scattered the ground like confetti in Times Square on New Year's Eve. I scrambled to pick them up and then she bent down beside me while she was laughing. "You think I'm going to take this 'bait'?" she said while she held up a wiggling worm in her hands. "What?" I replied. I appreciated her cheesy joke, but didn't know exactly what she meant by it. "I saw you eyeing me up like the last roll at a Thanksgiving meal," we both laughed, but I laughed a little more nervously. I guess I wasn't as smooth as I thought. "So are you going to?" she asked. "Going to what?" I said. "Going to take me fishing!" By this point all of the worms were back in the blue plastic container and we were standing face to face on the street corner with her brother looking on. A slight breeze caught her dress and it waved in the wind. Hair covered the side of her face and I wanted to brush it back, but my hands were still caked in dirt. She just stood there smiling at me while waiting for an answer. The fishing poles were resting in the back of the truck, but I was already hooked.

Living Part Of Life

It sat there on the dresser. One had to look past the photographs of her and her high school friends. Tucked away in the back corner by the stack of Fall Out Boy CD's was a jar of cash. Some call it a "rainy day" fund. She called it her living fund. No, she didn't need to pay rent or to buy groceries. No, this was her "get the heck out of her and go far away" money. Any money that she received from birthdays, holidays and a percentage of her tip money went into the jar. She promised herself that she'd experience many different places. She wanted to eat food with weird names. She wanted to order drinks that she could barely pronounce. Take pictures with strangers. While her friends were saving up for clothes, shoes and new phones, she was putting it towards that trip. She imagined as if the plane ticket were in her hands now, but then she peeked into the jar and it brought her back to reality. She still had a long way to go, but many miles ahead of her.

Two Raindrops In The Night

She was running in the rain. She pictures her trusty umbrella sitting on the counter just like an awkward teenager longing for a hand to hold. Her dress was splattered with water like a blank canvas being greeted by a bucket full of paint. Her friend's show had already started, but she had heard the first song played so many times in her living room that she could afford to miss the beginning.

He was running in the rain. Above him was a red umbrella fighting off the rain like a nerdy kid on a playground surrounded by bullies. He saw her running down the street as she was screaming and laughing at herself. A smile formed at the corner of his mouth and he knew that he had to introduce himself to this woman.

They met each other at the door and seemed like they had experienced different days. Her dress was dripping on the sidewalk and his shirt looked like it had just come out of the dryer. She looked down at herself and then up at him. "I could've used you a bit earlier," she said as she tried to wring out her striped dress. "Well, I'm all yours now," he said and the two of them made their way into the wrong concert. The miscalculated brought them together along with the help of a little rain.

A Soldier In Her Heart

When I lay by you, it gives me peace. When I lay by you, all of my thoughts and worries disappear. My mind drifts back to our time that we had together. Growing up, you always would pick me to be on your team first, even though it made your backyard buddies mad. You said I was "special." In third grade, you set down flowers on my desk that you picked on your way to class. You didn't stop to talk, but dropped them off and smiled at me when I looked back at you. I recognized some of those flowers from Mrs. Connor's front yard, but I wasn't going to say anything to you...or Mrs. Connor. My heart was slowly becoming yours. I started spending more and more time with you. In high school, we'd sneak up to the water tower at night and we would make up stories about the people living in the houses below us. We talked about how we never wanted to stop being young. We never wanted to stop dancing when we felt like it, holding each others hands, people watching when we were bored on a Sunday, and grabbing an ice cream cone to satisfy our sweet tooth. You kissed me that night and said that you were going to marry me someday. That someday came a month before you left to go overseas and fight in the war.

We got married in that church out in the country that wasn't big enough to hold all of our family and friends, but we made the most of it. As we sat up in bed the night of our wedding, we didn't know what the future was going to look like. When you'd be home or if we should start a family before you left. I was crying because I didn't know what I was going to do without you. You took my hands and looked me in the eyes and said, "As long as the sun is in the sky, everything is going to be all right." I can't help but to think about that night and about you as I lay here beside you with the sun soaking into my skin. It rushes over me like your hands and I find peace. I'm home again. You're home again.

A Night In

The glow of the TV brings the only light to the room.
They sit side by side on the couch with a blue
popcorn bowl resting in between the two of the them.
She reaches into the bowl and plucks the popcorn out
like the crane games at the arcade. Maintaining eye
contact with the screen as each piece finds its way
into her mouth. He breaks his attention with the TV
and turns over to her. She sits there in his XXL shirt
he won at the basketball game and a blanket wrapped
around her waist. He smiles. She notices. "What? Do
I have something on my face?" she says. "No," he
replies. "I just can't help but to smile when I look at
you." You see, to him, she's the prettiest girl in any
room whether she's dressed up or is sitting in the
kitchen with sweats on and a bowl of cereal on a
Saturday morning. Her laugh is his soul medicine.
She's the biggest trash talker to him when it comes to
competing and he eats it up. Would he be fine
without her in his life? Maybe, but he doesn't want to
know what that life is like. "You're a goof," she says
as she throws another handful of popcorn into her
mouth. He's no better off now than the butter that is
soaking into the popcorn. He's all hers.

ABOUT THE AUTHOR

Dalton Hessel was born in a small town in the north woods of Wisconsin called Hayward. He is the son of Gary and Stacey Hessel and step son to Lori Hessel. Dalton would tell you himself that he wasn't much of a reader growing up, but over the past five years he's fallen in love with books and writing them as well. Dalton is a senior at the University of Wisconsin – Eau Claire where he is well known around campus as "Buddy the Finals Week Elf". He's not sure how, but he was actually a featured story on the news for it. "Craziest thing that's ever happened to me," he said in an interview with himself. (All right, you've probably caught on by now that he's writing all of this stuff himself since this is a self published book.) Anyways, he appreciates you spending your hard earned dollars on his book. Feel free to stop him if you see him and chat with him. He wants to know if this whole human connection thing worked.